THIS CANDLEWICK BOOK BELONGS TO:

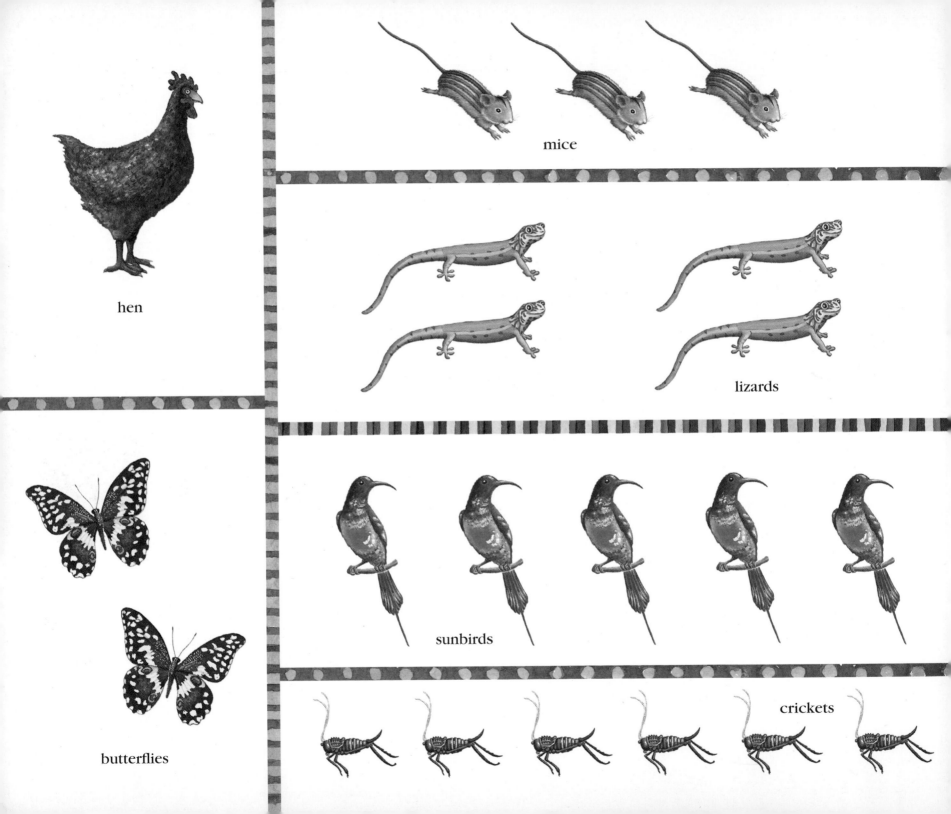

hen

mice

lizards

butterflies

sunbirds

crickets

baby bullfrogs

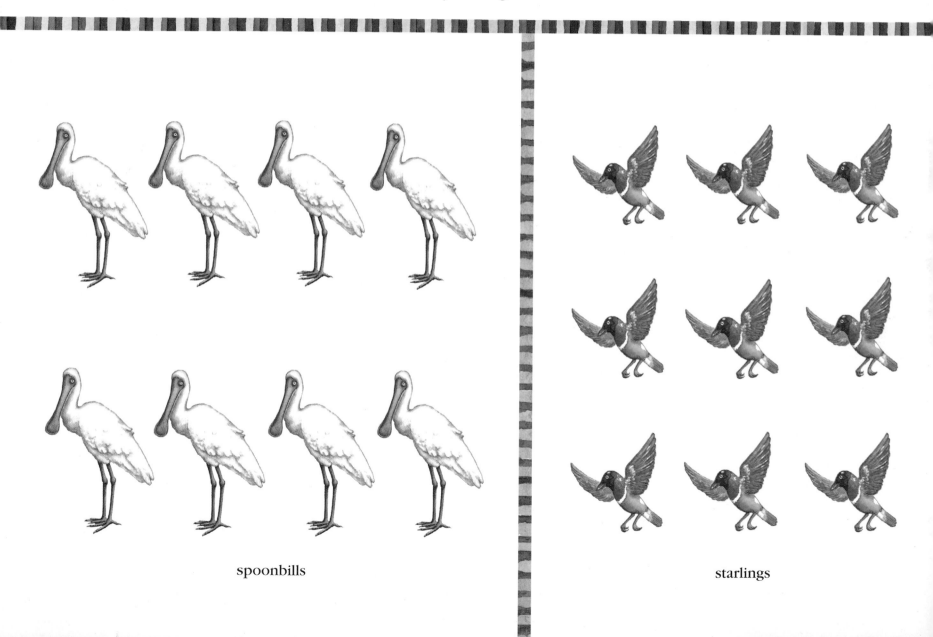

spoonbills

starlings

For John and Milo

The children featured in this book
are from the Luo tribe of southwest Kenya.
The author would like to thank everyone
who helped her research this book, in particular
Joseph Ngetich from the Agricultural Office
of the Kenya High Commission.

First U.S. edition 2011

Library of Congress Cataloging-in-Publication Data is available.

Library of Congress Catalog Card Number 2010051106

ISBN 978-0-7636-5361-3

17 18 19 20 SWT 10 9 8

Printed in Dongguan, Guangdong, China

This book was typeset in ITC Garamond.

Candlewick Press
99 Dover Street
Somerville, Massachusetts 02144

visit us at www.candlewick.com

HANDA'S HEN

EILEEN BROWNE

CANDLEWICK PRESS

Handa's grandma had one black hen.

Her name was Mondi, and every morning

Handa gave Mondi her breakfast.

One day, Mondi didn't come for her food.

"Grandma!" called Handa. "Can you see Mondi?"

"No," said Grandma. "But I can see your friend."

"Akeyo!" said Handa. "Help me find Mondi."

Handa and Akeyo hunted around the henhouse.

"Look! Two fluttery butterflies," said Akeyo.

"But where's Mondi?" said Handa.

They peered under a grain store.

"Shh! Three stripy mice," said Akeyo.

"But where's Mondi?" said Handa.

They peeked behind some clay pots.

"I can see four little lizards," said Akeyo.

"But where's Mondi?" said Handa.

They searched around some flowering trees.

"Five beautiful sunbirds," said Akeyo.

"But where's Mondi?" said Handa.

They looked in the long, waving grass.

"Six jumpy crickets!" said Akeyo. "Let's catch them."

"I want to find Mondi," said Handa.

They went all the way down to the water hole.

"Baby bullfrogs," said Akeyo. "There are seven!"

"But where's—? Oh, look! Footprints!" said Handa.
They followed the footprints and found . . .

"Only spoonbills," said Handa. "Seven . . . no, eight.
But where, oh where, is Mondi?"

"I hope she hasn't been swallowed by a spoonbill—
or eaten by a lion," said Akeyo.

Feeling sad, they went back toward Grandma's.

"Nine shiny starlings — over there!" said Akeyo.

"Listen," said Handa. cheep cheep "What's that?"

cheep cheep cheep cheep cheep cheep cheep cheep

"It's coming from under that bush," said Akeyo.

"Shall we peek?"

Handa, Akeyo, Mondi, and ten chicks

hurried and scurried and skipped back to Grandma's . . .

where they all had a very late breakfast.

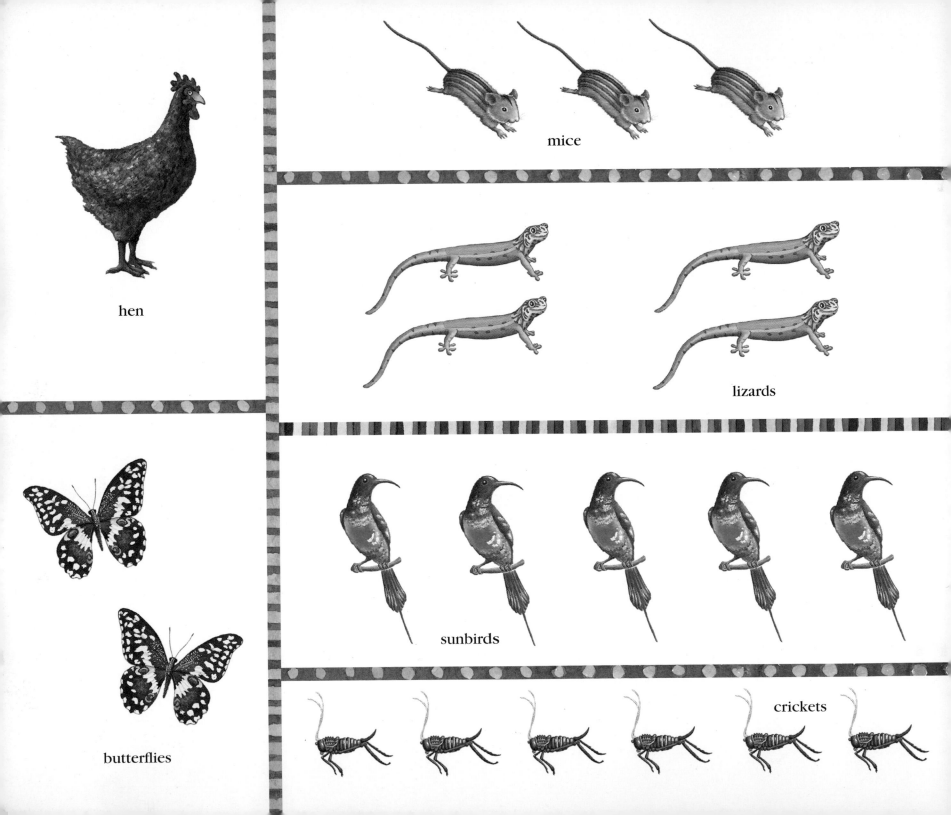

hen

mice

lizards

butterflies

sunbirds

crickets